The World's Longest Toenail

by Susan Knight

illustrated by Luke Jurevicius

Characters

Jake

Sam

Contents

Chapter 1

Hit and Miss

Jake loved going to the pool. He loved the water and his friends were always there. They splashed about and yelled a lot.

Between swims they lay under a tree and licked ice-creams.

"I wish this pool had a water slide," said Jake. "A water slide would be cool."

"Yeah!" said his friend Sam. "A really big one, with lots of twists and turns!"

Sam spread his arms to show how big.
He waved them around to show how many
twists and turns. His choc-mint ice-cream
flew off the cone. It hit Jake in the face.

Jake hated choc-mint. He tried to kick
Sam hard but Sam squirmed out of
the way.

Jake's toes crunched into the tree by
mistake. "Ow! Ow!" Jake cried.

Jake had to go to the doctor. His foot
was broken!

Chapter 2

Hopping Along

Jake hopped about with his foot in plaster for a long time. It was hot and itchy. Jake couldn't go to the pool.

At last the doctor cut off the plaster.
"Your foot is fine now," the doctor said.

Jake's mum looked at his foot. She pulled
a face. "Yuk! Look at those toenails!"

Jake's toenails had grown *very* long.

"I'll cut them for you," said the doctor.
He cut the little toenail.

"Ah! Aha ha ha ha ha!" Jake laughed.
"Stop! You're tickling! Stop!"

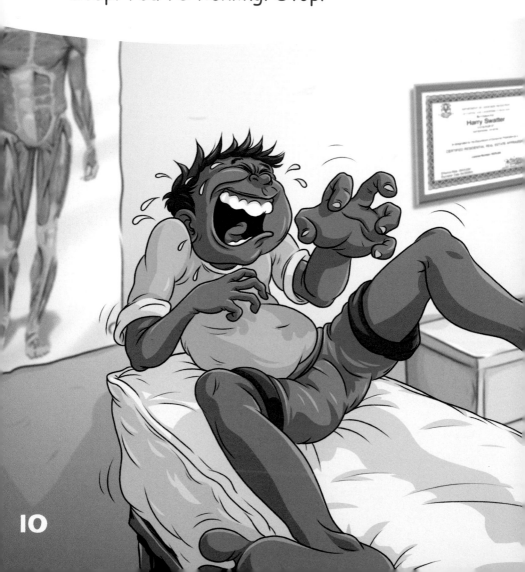

Jake pulled his foot away. This made the doctor cut his own tie in half. "You'd better go home," said the doctor. "Your father can do it for you."

Jake's dad had a go at the second
toenail. It still tickled.

"Oooh! Ohoo hoo hoo hoo hoo!" laughed
Jake.

He wriggled so much he kicked his dad on
the chin. His dad said a rude word.
Dad said, "Mum can do it for you!"

Jake's mum cut the third toenail. It still
tickled too much.

"Ee! Ee eee heee eeee!" Jake screeched.
He was so loud his mum got a headache.
She also broke a fingernail and that made
her crabby.
"Let your brother do it!" she snapped.

13

Jake's brother Alan did the fourth toenail. It tickled more than ever. That was until Alan clipped a piece out of Jake's toe as well.

"Haha hoho hee hee. Hey! Ow! Ow!" Jake roared.

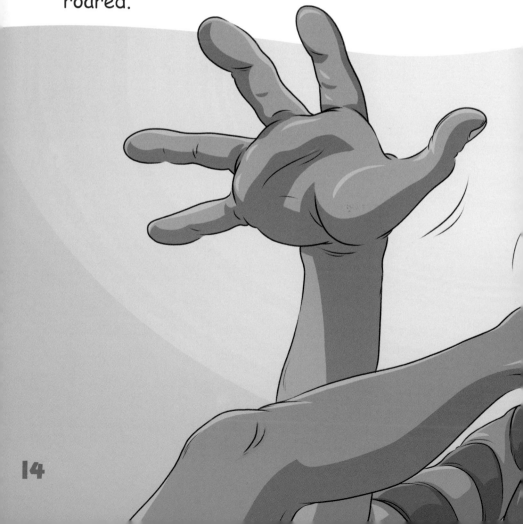

Jake jerked his foot and his big toe went up Alan's nose. Alan's nose began to bleed.

"That's enough!" Alan yelled, holding his nose. "You can cut the last one yourself!"

Chapter 3

The Last Toenail

Jake liked his last, long toenail. He didn't want to cut it. "I'm going to have the longest toenail in the world!" Jake said.

The toenail kept on growing. It grew longer every day. It ripped a hole in Jake's sheets.

It corkscrewed a hole out of his shoe.

Jake's mum made him a special, big toenail sock. She had to keep making the sock bigger and bigger. At last she gave up.

Jake was very proud of his toenail. He
trained it to twist up and around. He also
bent it down and used it like a pogo stick.
He could bounce all the way to school.

Jake became famous. His picture was in the papers. He was on TV. All the kids at school thought he was cool. He had the *Longest Toenail in the World!*

Chapter 4

Smelly and Stuck

One day a load of sacks fell off the back of a truck. They rolled and came to a stop on the footpath. Jake hopped around the corner straight onto one of the sacks.

Jake's toenail went PING! Jake spun around like a corkscrew. And there he stuck.

Everybody pushed and shoved. People with cameras took photos. People with notebooks asked questions.

"What does it feel like to be trapped by your toenail, Jake?" they asked.

The sacks were full of cow-poo fertiliser.
It smelt very nasty. The longest toenail
in the world was no fun anymore.

At last Jake got to the pool. He sat on the edge of the pool, feeling cross. He splashed his toenail in the water. It still smelt like cow poo.

Suddenly he felt a funny buzzing in his toe. The longest toenail in the world was growing.

Longer and wider and taller! And it was growing FAST!

It curled three times round his body. It shot past his ears. It twisted over his head. It snaked up past the diving board.

Jake gasped as his toenail snaked and grew. As big as himself ... as tall as a tree ... as big as a house ... as tall as a crane.

Chapter 5

Sam's Cool Idea

"Wow!" said Jake. He was now inside a huge cage of toenail. "That fertiliser is strong stuff!"

"Hey, Jake!" Sam called. "Don't worry, I'll get you out!"

Sam called the fire brigade.

The firefighters ran up their long
ladders. They tied the toenail steady
with ropes. They used special tools to
cut Jake free.

It still tickled but Jake shut his eyes and bit on a towel. He tried so hard he only kicked off two helmets.

The longest toenail in the world was free at last. "Good on you, Jake," said a firefighter.

Soon Jake and Sam and all the other kids were cheering. Now the pool has the longest, coolest, twistiest water slide in the world!

Glossary

corkscrewed
dug in a zigzag direction

crabby
cranky

fertiliser
manure to feed soil

plaster
stiff covering that helps broken bones heal

pogo stick
metal stick on a spring, used for jumping

snaked
moved and twisted like a snake

squirmed
wriggled

water slide
large, curving slippery dip with running water

Susan Knight

Here is the funniest thing that ever happened to me.

When my husband died he left mysterious chemicals in our house. So I asked a young science teacher I barely knew, to collect it for his school. When he came, he politely mentioned our nice view.

I put up my hand to wipe mist off the window — just as **he** bent forward to look out.

Somehow my fourth finger stuck straight up his nose!

Shock! Pain! Streaming eyes! Embarrassment!

I giggled all through my apology!

(Four years later the long-suffering man married me.)

Luke Jurevicius

"Some privacy please!"